Originally written and illustrated as:

Milo, the Tallest Leprechaun
Written and Illustrated
by: Emily Koenig

It is with the utmost pride that Emily's parents offer you the legacy their daughter left in this story. They sincerely hope you enjoy it and take its lessons to heart. In doing so, Emily will live on through you.

Milo, The Tallest Leprechaun, by Emily Grace Koenig

Copyright ' 2004 by Susan P. Koenig and Albert A. Koenig • Originally written and illustrated by Emily Grace Koenig in the year 2001

Published and released in 2004 by Little Treasure Publications

Cover and Interior Book Design by Pneuma Books, LLC. Visit www.pneumabooks.com

Body typeset in Cagliari 36 | 38 • Hardback version printed in Korea • Paperback version printed in the USA

Publisher's Cataloging-in-Publication
[Provided by The Donohue Group, Inc.]

Koenig, Emily Grace.
    Milo, the tallest leprechaun / [written and illustrated by] Emily Grace Koenig.
    p. cm.
    Cover title: The Tallest Leprechaun: a tall tale of terrible teasing
    ISBN: 0-9639838-6-5
    Leprechauns—Juvenile fiction. 2. Stature—Juvenile fiction. 3. Teasing—Juvenile fiction. 4. Social acceptance—Juvenile fiction.
  I. Title. II. Title: The tallest leprechaun : a tall tale of terrible teasing.

PS3561.03344   M55 2004
                          813 / .54—dc21

~~~~~~~~~~~~~~~~

Acknowledgments

Emily Grace Koenig died suddenly at age 12 from bacterial meningitis. On Emily's behalf, her parents, Susan and Albert Koenig, thank the following individuals and organizations for their support and assistance in bringing this special project to completion:

Mrs. Bonnie Sterling, Emily's 6th grade teacher, for inspiring her to write and re-write this story with her own style and artistic flair.

Sally Brown, Director of Peters Place in Berwyn, Pennsylvania, a center for grieving families, who led us to Little Treasure Publications.

Bernadette Garzarelli, Publisher and Paula Lizzi, Marketing Director of Little Treasure Publications for reviewing Emily's story, and encouraging us to pursue publishing her book. They have worked diligently and with sensitivity to make this book a reality.

Last, but not least, we wish to thank all of Emily's teachers and mentors, her many friends and all those who helped shape her into the exceptional young girl she became. Her life and inspiration live on in all of us.

Thank you, Paula, for your birthday wishes to Emily...
"Emily, today on your thirteenth birthday, July 8, 2003, you are the one giving the gifts.
Your book "The Tallest Leprechaun" is going to inspire thousands of children to look beyond a person's physical structure into their character, and into what makes them real, from the inside. You will also be responsible for thousands of children who will one day, like to become writers or illustrators. And because of you, your parents and many other champions will see to it that all parents are aware of the symptoms of meningococcal meningitis and the availability of a life saving vaccine."

I dedicate this book
to all those who are tall.
It may come in handy sometime!

–Emily Grace Koenig

4

Milo walked into the schoolroom in his hometown Dublin, Ireland to see all the other leprechauns staring at him.

a very
special
desk

Milo's desk
had to be specially made
because of his height.

Everyone makes fun of Milo,
especially Owen.

Even the teacher,
Mr. Lori laughs sometimes.

Milo is just too tall!

"Look guys, it's Milo. Everyone, say hi to Milo," Owen teases.

At that,
all of the other leprechauns said,

"Hilo Milo!"

Everyone,
including Mr. Lori
laughed hysterically.

mighty
mean
laugh

13

"All right, everyone hush,"
Mr. Lori yelled.

"Now, take out your homework
from last night," he continued.

Owen had a worried look
about his face.

16

"Owen, where is your work?"
Mr. Lori questioned.

"I-I-I-ahh-omm-I don't know.
It was here,"
Owen said in denial.

"Owen, go sign the book of the unlucky,"
Mr. Lori said angrily.

[The book of the unlucky
was where leprechauns
signed their names
if they forgot something for class.]

When Owen got home, he was still puzzled. "I wonder where my paper is?" he thought.

Suddenly,
with a large grin on his face,
he looked toward the top of his mighty high bookshelf.

"My paper!"

He was jumping up and down for what seemed like forever.

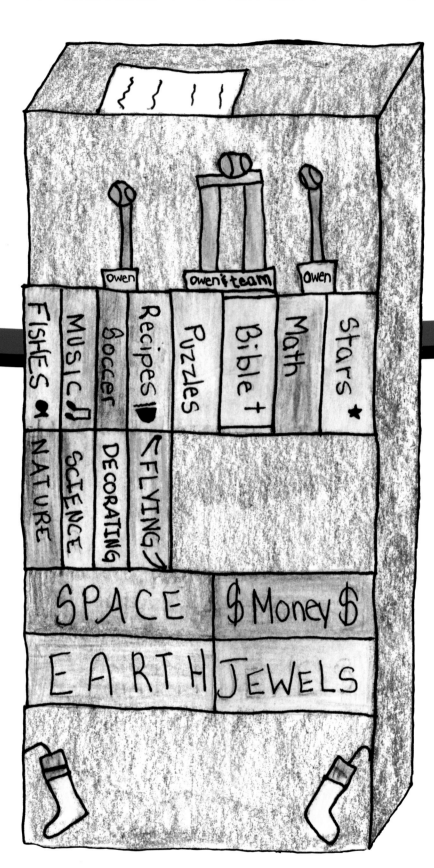

mighty high bookshelf

21

The next day at school, Mr. Lori asked Owen where his paper was.

Owen stuttered all over the place. "I-I-found-it-bu-but-I-c-can't r-reach it," he finally admitted.

If only...

heels

If only...

Springs

If only...

long legs

If only...

Stools

23

"I can get it for you," Milo said.
"R-r-really?" Owen questioned.
"Really," Milo reassured him.

That night,
Milo went over to Owen's house
and reached to the top of the
mighty high bookshelf.

"I got it!"

Milo said.
He gave Owen his paper
and said his goodbyes.

mighty long arm!

???

owen

Owen's team

owen

Recipes ♥
Soccer
MUSIC ♪
FISHES ●

Puzzles
Bible +
Math
Stars ★

FLYING
DECORATING
SCIENCE
NATURE

27

The next day at school,
Owen turned in his paper.
Mr. Lori was quite pleased.
Owen was happy too.

Owen learned his lesson of friendship and what it means to be a good person.

As for Milo, he learned that being tall is not a weakness, it's an advantage.

From that day on,
Owen and Milo
were best friends.

a very
special
rainbow
of friendship

About the Author

Emily Grace Koenig was born on July 8, 1990 or 7-8-9 as we have always remembered it. As a young child, Emily quickly bonded with a neighborhood friend, Alex, who became her playmate for life. She began her education at Brandywine Children's House, a Montessori school in Malvern, Pennsylvania. It was there that she learned to interact with boys and girls, and learned the powerful lesson of respect for human values. To this day, Emily is remembered as a compassionate child who lived this lesson every day of her life. Emily then attended The Montgomery School, a private co-ed grade school in Chester Springs, Pennsylvania, where she thrived in a culture of art, science, and diversity.

Fortunate to have been accepted to Villa Maria Academy in Malvern, Pennsylvania, Emily moved on to 5th grade where she found endearing friendships, a sustaining faith in God, and excelled academically, physically, emotionally and spiritually. In 6th grade Emily's language arts teacher, Mrs. Bonnie Sterling, gave the students an assignment to write and illustrate a story. She encouraged Emily to work and re-work her story, which resulted in this book, "The Tallest Leprechaun." Mrs. Sterling praised Emily's diligent attention to detail, her exceptional attitude, and her dream to one day become a teacher. She remained a mentor and inspiration to Emily in many ways.

Date Due
